HAUNTED HOUSE

HAUNTED HOUSE

by
Shirley Hughes

Prentice-Hall, Inc., Englewood Cliffs, New Jersey

HAUNTED HOUSE

Library of Congress Cataloging in Publication Data

Hughes, Shirley.
  Haunted house.

    SUMMARY: Two children are afraid to go near an ominous-looking old house until they learn its inhabitants, a little girl and her grandmother, are being held captive.
    n1. Mystery and detective storiesm   I. Title.
PZ7.H87395Hau 1978   nFicm   77-26814

0-13-384206-1

On the path by the railroad tracks, quite near to where Jim and Arthur lived, was a big house. It was a gloomy old place with high brick walls. The windows were boarded up and the gates always kept padlocked. Nobody went in and nobody came out, except for a big tom cat, as black as a shadow.

On one of the gateposts, carved in stone, was the name:

HARDLOCK HOUSE

There were spooks in there. Jim and Arthur knew this for sure because they had heard the ghostly screams.

Sometimes they dared one another to squeeze through the gate, where the bars had rusted away, and creep up the overgrown drive. Thick bushes grew on either side, dripping and rustling.

Round the corner, the drive opened out into a small garden where a crumbling porch tottered over the front door. There were little windows on either side of it with cracked panes of colored glass. But Jim and Arthur never got a closer look before the screaming started. It came from one of the windows, high and shrill.

"Go away, go away, go awayeeeeee..." it screamed.

Jim and Arthur never waited to find out what was going to happen next.

"It's a ghost!" little Arthur would say, his eyes wide with fright. "There's a horrible witch in there. Don't let's *ever* go there again, Jim."

But somehow neither of them could keep away for long.

Arthur had some scary thoughts about the house in his bed at night. Jim always pretended not to mind that sort of thing.

One day during vacation, when they were fooling
around on the footpath behind Hardlock House, they
spotted a foothold in the high brick wall at the back of
the house. Jim gave Arthur a boost and climbed up after
him. They both sat astride the wall, looking over
at the high windows beyond.
    All was quiet.

One of the windows was unshuttered. Suddenly a white face appeared, looking out at them! It was a young girl. They stared at each other silently. Then she beckoned, and was gone.

Jim and Arthur sat for a long time staring up at the empty window. Then they slid down on to the footpath and sat with their backs against the wall.

"Arthur," said Jim seriously, "that wasn't a spook. It was a girl. This is a real mystery."

"Yes," said Arthur. *"But it's too frightening for me!"*

Jim was frightened too, but he didn't let Arthur know.

Jim and Arthur's Mom had once read them a story about a girl who was shut up in a tower by a wicked witch. They thought a great deal about the face at the window of Hardlock House.

Next day they watched from the wall for a long time, but no face appeared. Then Jim noticed a basement door at the bottom of a flight of steps, where the shutter had come off and a glass pane was broken.

Jim slithered down into the yard and tried the door. It opened! Putting his finger to his lips, Jim made signs to Arthur to stay where he was. Then he disappeared into the house.

Poor Arthur! He badly wanted to run home, but he couldn't desert his brother. After a long while, he too climbed softly down into the yard and, trembling all over, crept in through the basement door to look for Jim.

Inside the house was a long passage, which smelled unpleasantly damp. There were empty storerooms on either side, with high, barred windows which let in a little dreary light.

Up a shadowy flight of stairs and into a large hall crept
Arthur, expecting to be pounced upon at any moment.

There were a great many doors leading off the hall.
Arthur paused. He heard voices. He peeped through the
crack in one of the doors. Then he opened it a tiny bit, and
a little wider, and peered around...

...and there, as large as life, was that cheeky Jim! He wa sitting on the floor, in a roo full of furniture muffled in dust sheets, talking to the blond girl. He had forgotten all about Arthur!

Arthur felt like punching Jim but he couldn't because Jim was bigger than he was

Besides, he wanted to find out about this girl. She looked rather nice, though a little skinny. She was certainly not a spook.

Jim started to explain. "This is Mary, and she..."

But at that moment the terrible ghostly screaming was heard in the hall. It was just outside the door!

In rushed a bony figure, all in black with wild white
hair, waving its stick-like arms about and gobbling like a
goose in between the screams.

"Go away—AAAAH—go away—SHRIEK—I'll have no
lads in here—AAAAUGH, gobble, gobble, gob—get out,
GET OUT!!"

Jim and Arthur both dived under a dust sheet and
crouched there, like a couple of ghosts themselves.

They were trapped.

But Mary was speaking calmly.

"Come on, Gran, behave. What about a cup of tea?"

It wasn't a witch. It was Mary's Granny, but she was very nearly as frightening. Peeping out from their sheet, Jim and Arthur saw Mary take her hand.

Slowly the screaming stopped. Mary managed to coax the old lady down to the kitchen and sat her in her chair. Not knowing quite what to do, Jim and Arthur followed, and stood about sheepishly.

While Granny sipped her tea, still gobbling and mumbling into her cup, Mary explained that she was having one of her "fits." She always had them when anyone came near the house. She couldn't stand visitors, because she mistook them for people from the Agency coming to ask questions and make her fill out difficult forms. This set her off in a screaming fit. She never went out, and didn't like Mary to go out either. Even the grocery man had to leave their boxes of food at the gate.

Pretty odd, I call it

Mary told Jim and Arthur that she and Granny had come from far away in the country to be caretakers at Hardlock House. They had found the job through an ad in the paper. The owner of the house, Captain Grimthorpe, was never there. In fact, Granny had only seen him once, though a painting of him hung in the hall in a big gold frame. He looked very grand, with bushy ginger hair and whiskers.

Now he had gone off traveling and it seemed he had forgotten all about them, for he never sent any money for repairs. It worried them.

Mary was an orphan. She and Granny had only each other in all the world. Although they loved each other very much, Mary was bored and lonely without friends of her own age. School hadn't begun yet, and there was nothing to do but to sit at the window and watch the trains go rattling by. Her only companion was the black cat, Uriah. She begged Granny to let Jim and Arthur come and see her sometimes.

After that the three children often played together. Sometimes Jim and Arthur even offered to help Granny sweep up, and went around trying to fix things for her.

One afternoon they found Mary and Granny both in tears. It was over Mary's clothes. She had to wear grown-ups' old ones, cut down for her by Granny.

"How can I go to a new school in these things?" sobbed Mary. "All the others will laugh at me."

Jim and Arthur thought it strange to cry over a thing like clothes. But they had to admit that although Granny had done her best, Mary didn't look quite like other girls. Her skirts were too long and limp, and her shoes looked funny. They decided to see what they could do.

When they arrived at Hardlock
House a few days later with a big
box of secondhand clothes, Mary
was so delighted that she put them
all on at once and danced about all
over the room. Jim and Arthur were
so pleased with themselves.

Even Granny cheered up a bit.

But then a terrible thing happened. One evening Jim and Arthur were coming up the drive, when they both stopped short, staring at the lighted window ahead. Against the closed blind was the shadow of an enormous man!

24

Jim and Arthur didn't know quite what to do. After a while they went around to the back door and knocked timidly. Immediately there was a great noise of barking and the door was flung open by a fat man with ginger curls and whiskers, holding a villainous looking red-eyed dog on a leash.

Behind him in the passage they could see Mary and Granny, clinging together.

"What the devil do you want?" the man shouted. "I won't have boys knocking at my door! Take yourselves off before I set the dog on you!"

Jim and Arthur were too surprised to do anything but obey.

The next day they hung around on the footpath until at last Mary put her head over the wall. She looked unhappy and had been crying.

She told them that the owner of the house,
Captain Ginger Grimthorpe, had returned
suddenly. He was very cross about the state of the
place, and was threatening to send them away.
Then they would be homeless! What was more, he
did nothing but shout at them, and his dog kept
barking at Uriah.

Now Jim and Arthur were never allowed to see
Mary. She had very little chance to play anyway,
since she had to spend so much time doing
housework and helping Granny look after Captain
Grimthorpe. He was very demanding and sat about
grumbling all day.

Poor Granny was quite worn out with all the work, and running up and down stairs.
But worse was to come.

Uriah had a big fight
with Captain Grimthorpe's
red-eyed dog.

He chased him all over the house and
scratched him badly on the nose.

Captain Grimthorpe said that he wouldn't
have that badly behaved cat around the place
any longer, and he locked Uriah in an upstairs
room.

He was to be sent away to an animal shelter in
the morning!

Jim and Arthur looked very grave
when they heard this news. They liked Uriah
very much; he was such a good fighter.

"Don't worry," said Jim,
"we'll save him somehow."

He was a very
resourceful boy.

Together they thought of a plan. Mary was to get
the key to the room in which Uriah was imprisoned.
This was difficult, as it hung on a hook in the hall,
just outside Captain Grimthorpe's sitting room.
But Captain Grimthorpe always ate and drank
too much at suppertime and went off to sleep
in a chair with his mouth open. The red-eyed
dog did the same, stretched out on the rug.

Neither of them heard
Mary as she slipped gently
into the hall, took
the key, and crept
upstairs.

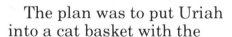

It's only me, Uriah dear, I've come to save you.

The plan was to put Uriah into a cat basket with the

You won't be inside for long, I promise.

lid firmly fastened on, and to lower him out of the window on a long rope,

to the boys who would be waiting in the yard below.

miaow!

Uriah was very pleased to see Mary but he didn't much care for the cat basket.
At last he was safely inside.

Leaning out, Mary
could see Jim and Arthur's
upturned faces in
the dark below the
window. The basket
wobbled on its rope
as she started to lower
it. Half way down,
Uriah decided he'd
had enough.

He started to turn
round and round inside,
miaowing and scratching
at the lid. The basket
swung about wildly,
banging against the
sitting room window.

A light shone out.
The window was thrown
open, and Captain Grimthorpe
put his head out, peering
into the darkness.

Who's there?

At that moment Uriah's nose appeared under the lid
of the basket. In no time he had forced his way out and,
clinging on for a moment with his claws, he made a
great leap, landing right on top of Captain Grimthorpe's
head!

There was a great uproar of wild cries and curses,
and a flurry of ginger curls. Uriah tore off into the
night, wearing a ginger wig—and Captain Grimthorpe
was quite bald!

Then a great many confusing things seemed to
happen at once. They all crowded into the hall.
Granny ran out of the kitchen, throwing her apron
over her head and making a noise like a mad owl.
Bald Captain Grimthorpe stamped about, purple in
the face with rage, calling for his wig. Mary was
crying, "Oh, Uriah, come back, come back!" And the
red-eyed dog barked fiercely at everybody.

At this moment little Arthur stepped bravely forward, and said in a calm, clear voice:

"Captain Grimthorpe doesn't look a bit like his portrait up there without his hair on. I don't think he's the same man at all!"

There was a sudden silence. Granny came out from under her apron and peered into Captain Grimthorpe' face.

"My goodness, I do believe the boy is right. You're not the gentleman I remember—I can see that now, even without my glasses."

"His moustache doesn't look very real either,"
observed Jim, "It's sort of coming loose on one side."

Captain Grimthorpe's face flushed scarlet, and so did his shiny bald head. Muttering something under his breath, he retreated upstairs with his red-eyed dog at his heels.

"I always thought there was something funny about him," said Mary. "But don't let's bother about him now, the horrid old thing. We've *got* to find Uriah."

For a long time they searched and called. It seemed hours before they heard an answering miaow, and Uriah came strolling up, shaking his back legs, and pretending that nothing unusual had happened.

The next day Granny had some news for them. Captain Grimthorpe had disappeared! He had packed his things in the night and gone off with his dog, leaving nothing behind but a false moustache on the dressing table.

Of course, he wasn't the real Captain Grimthorpe at all. It turned out that he was the Captain's lazy brother, Maurice, well known for his bad temper and dishonesty, who was going about in disguise to avoid paying his debts. Uriah had revealed his secret. Neither he nor his dog were ever seen again in those parts.

Soon afterwards some social workers from the Agency called. As soon as Granny saw them, she let out a shriek, and threw her apron over her head again. But they were politely trying to explain that Hardlock House was to be made into an Old People's Home, with the agreement of the *real* Captain Grimthorpe, and that Granny was to be one of the first to be offered a place there.

It's all right, Gran.

So Granny soon settled down to a new life, having her meals cooked for her, playing Bingo, and watching programs on color TV. She even got used to the other old people, though she sometimes complained about them.

And Mary?

Jim and Arthur had grown so fond of her that she came to live at their house as one of the family, and they all started school together when the term began. Uriah had already made himself at home, without being asked.

As for the ginger wig, which Uriah had abandoned on a fence down by the railway footpath, it hung there forgotten all winter, blowing about in the wind. But when the spring came a couple of sparrows made a nest in it, and settled down to raise a family.

THIS IS NOT THE END!
(please turn over)

Now that you've read this story, you might like to try acting it out in a group. You can make up your own parts, and add in anything extra you can think of.

You'll need at least six people. The names with the stars against them can be left out, or acted by the same people.

CHARACTERS
Jim.
Arthur.
Mary.
Granny.
Captain Grimthorpe.
Uriah, a cat.
Captain Grimthorpe's red-eyed dog.
People from the Agency.*
Old people.*
Grocery man.*

Costumes aren't essential, but it would be more fun if you could get hold of:
A wig.
An apron for Granny.
Some clothes for Mary to try on.
A tray with cups and plates.
A cardboard carton with a lid for Uriah's cat basket.

Of course the scene where Mary lowers Uriah out of the window will have to be imagined from the point of view of the boys waiting below.